J
PIC
HAC

Hachler, Bruno.

What does my teddy
bear do all day?

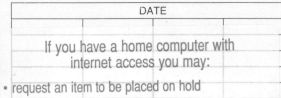

a minedition book
published by Penguin Young Readers Group

Text copyright © 2004 by Bruno Hächler
Illustrations copyright © 2004 by Birte Müller
Coproduction with Michael Neugebauer Publishing Ltd. Hong Kong.

Published simultaneously in Canada.
Manufactured in Hong Kong by Wide World Ltd.
Designed by Michael Neugebauer
Typesetting in Veljovic, designed by Jovica Veljovic.
Color separation by Fotoreproduzioni Grafiche, Verona, Italy.

Library of Congress Cataloging-in-Publication Data available upon request.

ISBN 0-698-40003-8
10 9 8 7 6 5 4 3 2 1
First Impression
For more information please visit our website: www.minedition.com

What Does My Teddy Bear Do All Day?

By Bruno Hächler
with pictures by
Birte Müller

Translated by
Charise Myngheer

minedition

I love my teddy bear!

Does he sit upon my pillow...
not make a single sound?
Or does he jump upon my mattress,
running all around?

My teddy bear seems really sweet,
but maybe I've been fooled.
I wonder what he does all day
when I am off at school.

Does he listen to my radio
and dance with my best doll?
Or think up crazy pictures
and paint them on the wall?

I think that I will stay at home
and spy on him today.
I'll find out everything he does
when I have gone away!

You wait. I'm gonna catch you!

As I peeked out from my covers,
he didn't seem to care.
He may have seen me watching,
'cause he didn't move a hair.

You wait. I'm gonna catch you!

When I spied through my small keyhole
to see if he would move,
he just sat there very sweetly
and didn't leave a clue.

You wait. I'm gonna catch you!

I stared through my own window
so he would never know.
But he was smart and sat there stiff
and watched me like a crow.

You wait. I'm gonna catch you!

I turned the music way up loud
and snuck across the floor.
He didn't even blink an eye
as I hid behind the door.

You wait. I'm gonna catch you!

The TV played his favorite show.
I left it on all day.
But he didn't even turn his head
or try to look that way.

You wait. I'm gonna catch you!

I have just one more plan to try.
I don't think I can miss.
I'll open up the honey jar—
I know he can't resist.

And now I'm gonna catch you!

Oh, no! You're gone!

Where are you, little teddy bear?
I know you must be here.
Your tricks are good, but we both know
you cannot disappear!

And there you sit.

Your belly is completely full...
I bet you couldn't stop.
The honey jar is empty now...
and you're about to pop!

See...I caught you!